BEAR LIKES JAM

Ciara Gavin

Alfred A. Knopf 🐎 New York

For Jerome and Edwin

THIS IS A BORZOI BOOK PUBLISHED BY ALFRED A. KNOPF

Copyright © 2017 by Ciara Gavin

All rights reserved. Published in the United States by Alfred A. Knopf, an imprint of Random House
Children's Books, a division of Penguin Random House LLC, New York.
Knopf, Borzoi Books, and the colophon are registered trademarks of Penguin Random House LLC.

Visit us on the Web! randomhousekids.com
Educators and librarians, for a variety of teaching tools, visit us at RHTeachersLibrarians.com

Library of Congress Cataloging-in-Publication Data is available upon request.
ISBN 978-0-399-55179-6 (trade)
ISBN 978-0-399-55180-2 (lib. bdg.)
ISBN 978-0-399-55181-9 (ebook)

MANUFACTURED IN CHINA
February 2017
10 9 8 7 6 5 4 3 2 1   First Edition

When Bear tasted jam for the first time,
he couldn't believe what he'd been missing.

Bear liked jam *so* much, he forgot
to share it with the ducks.

Sometimes Bear even snuck jam when he knew he wasn't supposed to.

Mama Duck was worried. Big bears
need a balanced diet, she said.

So Bear showed her how well he could balance.
But Mama Duck was firm: no more jam until
Bear ate his vegetables.

At dinner, strange green things appeared on Bear's plate. Bear poked it.

He piled it.

He flattened it out.

But he was very, *very* careful not to taste any of it.

Bear couldn't take it anymore. If he didn't have some jam soon, he was sure he would become seriously ill.

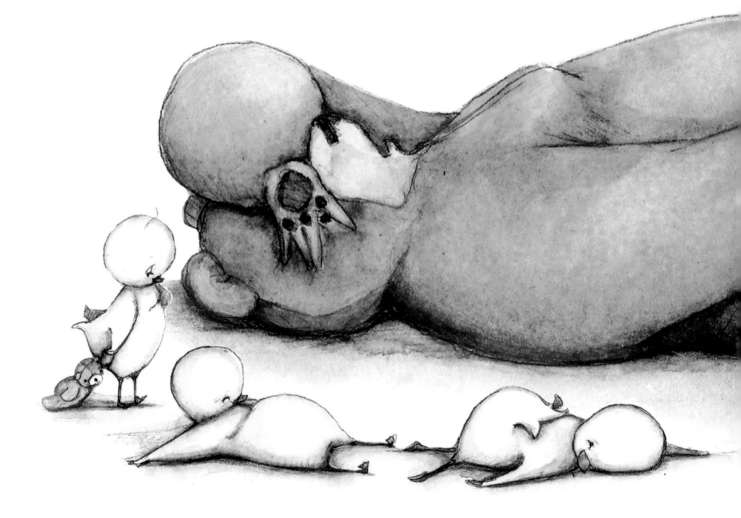

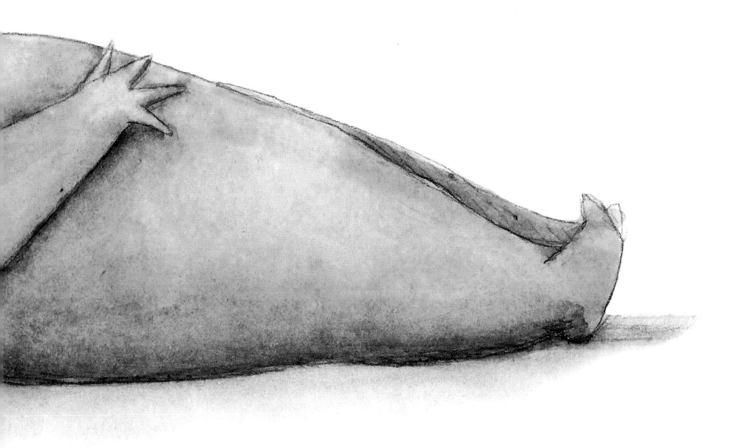

That night, Bear's tummy growled
so loudly he couldn't sleep.

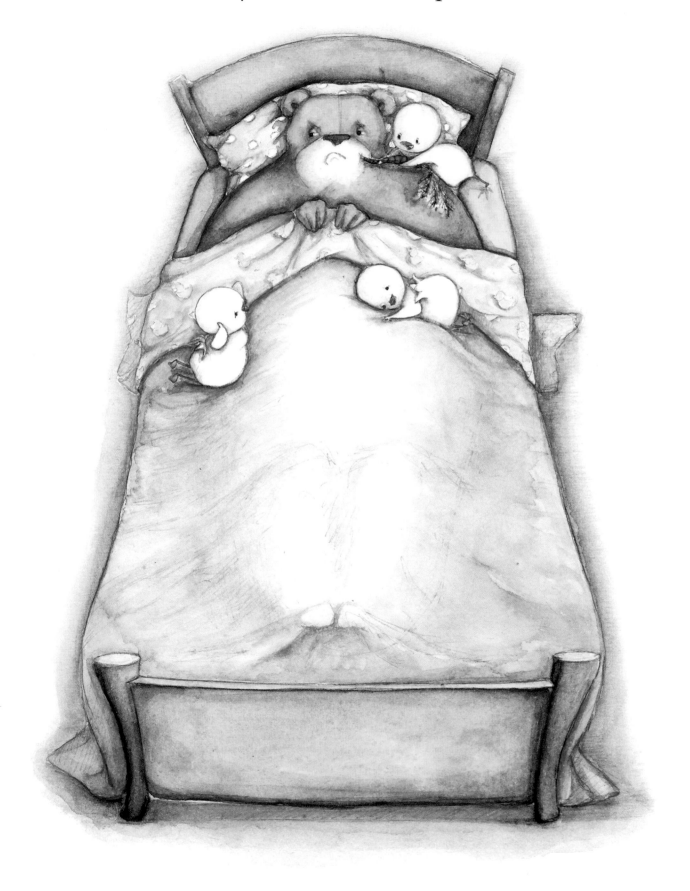

The next morning, Bear looked for jam.
But breakfast was oatmeal.

There was no jam at dinner, either.

But there *was* a game.
And Bear loved games.

First, Boy Duck showed them how to stick a pea to their noses with jam. The first one to lick it off won. Bear won five times in a row.

Next, Girl Duck showed them how to bury their corn under a mountain of mashed potatoes. Then the race was on to dig up the gold. Bear found his corn first.

Before he knew it, Bear had eaten
all of his vegetables.

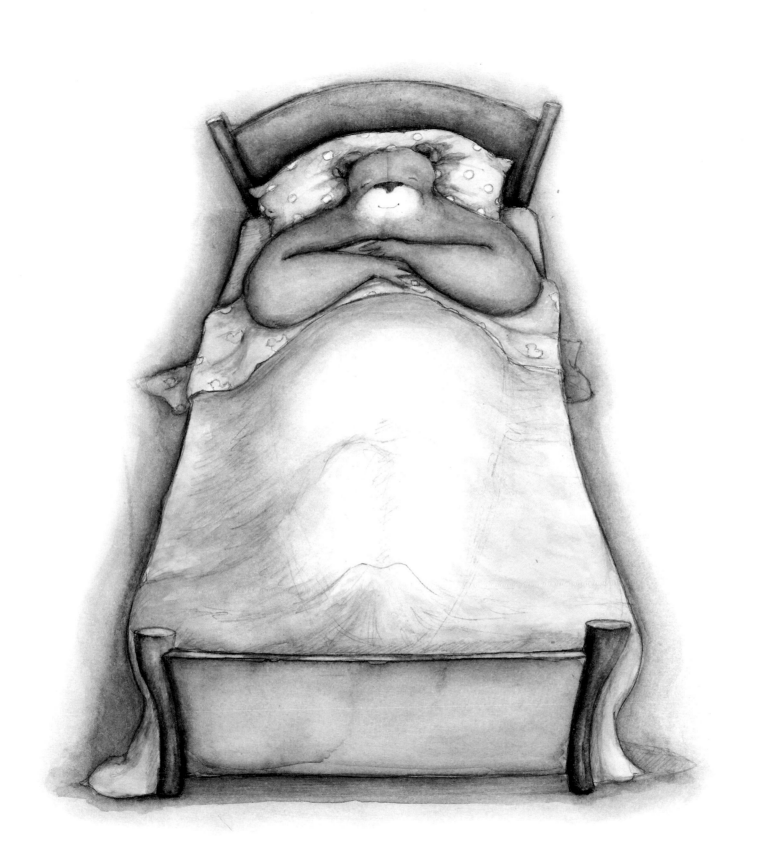

And when he went to bed, his tummy
didn't grumble at all.

Now Bear eats vegetables every night.
And for balance . . .

he likes to share a jar (or two)
of jam with the ducks.